ALYSSA'S BEAUTY WITHIN

BY CHRISTOPHER C SMITH

Christopher C. Smith

Father, Author, Actor, Independent Publisher & Song Writer

Thanks and Dedications

First and foremost I would like to give thanks to the Almighty God.

My beautiful mother Ora Henderson

My beautiful daughter Lauren Smith

LaTasha

Neme Cancel

Quinn De Leon

The whole PBF family

I would also like to thank Moe Dirdee

Nikki

Amy

I would also like to thank the whole EGM team.

Cas Youngstar

Jerm

Dj Lont

Shacora Johnson

Christopher Bullock

I would also like to thank

Darrell Washington

Jordan Loya

Erik Felix

Cash Blocka & B.G.G

Nafeesa Peoples

The whole Yonkers, New York family

Mrs. Carrie

#5404 thanks for all the love & support

And anyone else I have forgotten, I thank you.

Nafeesa's Day Spa

First of all I must say as the owner of Nafeesa's Day Spa & Wellness Center that I am very excited to be a sponsor of this intriguing, remarkable book "Alyssa's Beauty Within". I believe that every reader of this book will enjoy the book & it's entirely. I'm very proud of this Author Christopher C. Smith who is doing a wonderful job with reaching men, women, children and young adults. Nafeesa's Day Spa & Wellness Center is located @ 7667 w. 95th St #1E Hickory Hills, Il 60457 (708)357-7641 spa (630)248-3297 business cell we offer the following services...manicures, pedicures, massages of all kind (ex. Swedish, hot stone, deep tissue, aromatherapy etc) foot detoxification, eyelashes, facials, waxing, body wrapping & chair massage. However if u bring in a copy of this book you get $10 off. Or mention the Author Christopher Smith. We also sale gift certificates that are good for 90 days and we do fundraising for organizations & individuals. You can find us on fb @ Nafeesa's Day Spa... inside of the Spa there is a boutique London Mo'Lan's Accessories which we have leather purses, custom rhinestone T-shirts, fashionable sunglasses, scarves, jewelry, swimsuits & shoes. Check us out on fb @ London Molan Accessories & londonmolanaccessories on Instagram... last but not least spread the word about this fantastic book Alyssa's Beauty Within! God bless.

Chapter 1

Finding Me

Ring, ring, ring!!! The bell rings as I lift my head from
waking up after falling asleep during my --fourth period class.
"Hope you guys have all the notes that were given in today's
class for tomorrow test", said Mrs. Smith, our Math teacher.
Lifting my head slowly as I look around staring and wiping my
mouth from the drool I had from taking a quick nap. I started
getting up and shaking my left leg, which had fallen asleep as
well. I then heard a small light whisper in my ear saying, "Are
you ok? You were snoring kind of loud." "Ha ha, whatever" I
replied with a smirk on my face. Only to know that the whisper I
heard was the cutest guy in the class named Charles. He had the
most amazing smile and cutest eyes enough to make any girl in
the world fall for him at the drop of a dime. But with a girl like
me I knew I wasn't his type. So as I packed my entire stack of
books together and started heading out, walking aside of me,
Charles opened the door and I charmingly said, "Thank you.
You're so kind." Strolling down the aisle to my fifth period class,
which was my last class. Dragging my feet, sluggishly walking,
still sleepy from going to bed at 3:45 am from watching music
videos and America's Next Top Model hoping one day to
become as successful and beautiful as the models that contend

and fight to win a modeling contract and hopefully I can become as successful as my idol Beyoncé.

As I finally reached the door to my fifth period class I take a deep breath and sigh. Reciting to myself "Ugh, here we go again." as I reach for the knob. I then felt a warm hand cover mines saying, "I got you." I began to realize it was Charles from my previous fourth period class. So without any hesitation slowly pulling my hand away and allowing him to open the door as he replied again with a smirk looking at me up and down saying, "ladies first." As I turn to him with the same smirk as he had given me replying "Thank you!" "Before you sit down please turn in yesterday's Five-Paragraph Essay that is due today on my desk." yelled my favorite English teacher Mrs. Davis. Walking into her class I headed slowly over to her desk turning in the homework just as she insisted. After doing so I headed towards my assigned seat still sluggish and sleepy I began to trip over my own two feet, catching myself on my best friend's Nicole's desk. "Ha, ha, ha" she giggled before asking, "Are you ok?" "Yes." with a smile I reply. Nicole then replies with a smirk and says, "Are you sure, too much drinking last night? Ha! Ha! Ha!" "Yeah, okay! My father would kill me if he knew I had only taken a sip or a taste of liquor, or had done drugs for that matter." So with no hesitation I quickly sat down in my assigned seat which was right behind Nicole and two seats away from my other friend who I was soon to find out was also my second-cousin on my mother's Rae's side. Her name I believe was Chanel. I'm not quite sure, seeing as though we rarely ever spoke only in class and a little during gym. Setting my books down and resting my head I started to fall asleep again catching myself "Nope! Not this time." So as I begin to stare quietly at the black board, the bell initiating that class was about to begin had rang. Mrs. Davis begins to talk and teach starting today's lesson she had previously prepared for us. "Now students please tell me who is the author of one of the best poems ever written Still I Rise?" as Chanel raised her hand quickly while speaking confidently "Maya Angelou!" "Correct!" Mrs. Davis replied with a smile on her face. Now students remove everything from your desk and get ready for a surprise pop quiz "Ughhhh" the class recited in unison. As I started to prepare as instructed to I quickly remembered I forgot I didn't pack a single writing utensil. Thinking to myself, I must've left my pens and pencils in my previous class. Looking around seeing who might have an extra pen or pencil I can use for the moment. I felt a slight tap on my shoulder looking back to see what it was. To my surprise it was Charles giving me a pencil he had to spare. I quickly replied, "Thank you sooooo much." He then quickly replied quietly with a gentle laugh and smirk "No problem". I then turned back around and before my eyes I realized at my surprise the packet from the pop quiz Mrs. Davis had promised appeared to be so thick with a bright smile on her face she then said now students begin and please no cheating or looking around at other's papers!!!

I then slowly looked down starring at the first question on the test and took a deep breath and began what seems to be a 40 plus question surprise test that Mrs. Davis prepared for us. I then quickly began to work. Slowly for surely as I finished the test the bell rings to go home saying to myself "saved by the bell" as Mrs. Davis replies at a high pitched voice yelling at the top of her lungs "now students pens and pencils down" and as you guys leave please turn in your test as you head out and go straight home. Feeling relief and confident as I'm packing up and getting ready to turn in my test and get my books and other belongings together. I returned the pencil I had barrowed back to Charles. With a smirk on my face I replied thank you you're a life saver. As he then looks back at me as we make eye to eye contact with a cocky look on his face he then replies "I know I am". With the biggest grin and my head held back I quickly replied Ha! Ha! Ha! You're funny. Heading more than half way home on the school bus I then started to stare out the window while feeling every bump in the road. I then began day dreaming about seeing myself as beautiful as my idol Beyoncé but right before I can really imagine and get into deep thought the bus comes at an extremely complete hard stop. Jerking my head and quickly moving my book bag to the floor. To my surprise while picking up my book bag and looking back at the window I realized that the stop the bus driver had stopped at was my stop. So without any hesitation I quickly got off the bus and then walked right into my house, straight in to my room. How was school today my mom asked with a drowsy response "its fine ma" just a little tired. Already settled in my bed and under the covers ready to finish my nap from 4th period, my mom then opened my bedroom door slowly and asked "any homework"?? With my back to the door And half way sleep I replied "no mom just extra tired". With a happy response my mom replied "ok, dear dinner will be ready within an hour". I'm making your favorite "roast beef" and "macaroni and cheese". I then rolled over with the cheesiest smile and said thanks mom. I will be down shortly after my nap. "Ok Hun" my mom replied. "See you in a little." After an hour and a half passed I slowly wake up feeling highly rejuvenated. I then begin to place my feet on the cold bed room floor. Putting on my pink bunny slippers, I start heading down the stairs with the fresh smell of roast beef and macaroni and cheese hitting my nose at full speed. I quickly ran down the stairs and fallowed the smell where it led me to an empty chair and a plate of food. With my mom and dad already waiting, have a seat my dad replied. Hurry hun your food is getting cold my mom said with her gentle voice. I quickly sat down as we all bowed our heads and said a quick prayer. Slowly lifting my head I quickly grabbed my fork and knife and began stuffing my face with this delicious meal that placed before me. "Slow down" my dad said jokingly, as I gently laughed what's for dessert I asked with an exciting smile. My mom replied "7up cake". With my plate more than half way done I asked for seconds. So how was your day my mom asked while staring at me as if I did something wrong. "My day was fine" as I wiped the sauce from the meal off my face. I took a deep breath and begin asking my mom about my insecurities. Sounding disturbed and upset, mom why am I so skinny? And why do I have to be so unattractive? The other girls around me are popular. They get all the attention. Should I start putting tissue in my bra? Should I get cosmetic surgery?? Then out of nowhere with a very nervous and upsetting look my dad replied in a very serious voice "you are perfectly fine" everything about you is priceless. You're smart and intelligent. You have the prettiest set of eyes in the world. You are my angel. And don't ever let me hear you talk like that ever again "you hear me". With my head hanging down I gently and softly replied thanks dad. But in my head it was like his words went in one ear and out the other. Knowing that it was my father that was speaking to me and saying things he was supposed to say. I then started heading upstairs and into bed going back to sleep for school tomorrow.

RING RING RING!!!! As the sound from my alarm clock which was loud enough to wake up the neighbors woke me up right away. I started getting ready for school today. Rushing out the house my mom yells from the basement where she seemed to be doing laundry "Have a good day dear. Please don't forget your lunch on the counter by the toaster." Looking around nervously I grabbed the brown paper bag which had my name "Alyssa's lunch" written on it with big black letters. I then replied yelling "thanks ma, you're the greatest". Heading to school looking outside the window I hear a gentle voice whisper and calmly in my ear saying "Good morning beautiful". Looking back shockingly is my biggest crush Charles. After seeing those dreamy eyes and beautiful smile I replied "Thanks". He then set next to me which quickly melted my heart instantly. I then slowly looked the other way so he wouldn't see me blush. "Ughhh, here we go again" I said seeing the bus I was on pull up right in front of the school. I quickly got off and entered the school. Straight to my locker still feeling amazed that the guy I had a serious crush on has finally noticed me and called me beautiful. I then quickly rushed to my first period class which was social studies, a class in which I could care less about. But need the credit from the class in order to walk across the stage next year. As the day goes by still feeling some sort of butterflies from the comment that Charles had given me. I noticed that the time was going by fast. And before I knew it, It was already 5th period. Sitting in my desk taking notes in my note pad that Mrs. Davis had given to us to get ready for our next big test in a couple days. I felt a sharp poke in my left arm I nervously turned around rubbing my arm to see what it had happened. "Do you want to go out", Charles asked? With a gentle smile I then replied I would have to get permission. So with no hesitation Charles quickly slips me a note which seems to be his cell phone number. I turned around ripped off a small piece of notebook paper and begin to write my number down. Even more nervous than ever I slipped my number in return. Due to my surprise Charles had the biggest grin he replied "thanks".

RING, RING, RING!!!! The bell rings as the school day come to an end. I then packed all my belongings and headed straight to my bus with much excitement. I then text the number Charles had given me and said "how are you sir and how was your day"? With not even a few seconds gone by he then replied "I'm fine, how was yours". "Mine was fine, did you really think I was beautiful" I replied back. Texting back Charles said "Yes, you are gorgeous one of the best looking females in the school I must say". With a big cheesy smile I looked at my phone thinking Wow my dad was right. I guess I'm not as bad looking as I once thought. Seeing that the bus had come to a complete stop right in front of my house. I then walk towards the bus door and start heading home. I opened the front door seeing my mom and dad walking back and forth. I said "hi mom & dad" with a big smile on his face my dad replied "you're in such a good mood today". With my mom adding "oh yea how was your day? I replied "it was wonderful". Then shortly after I quickly asked "what's for dinner"? With a confused look on his face my dad replied "either pizza or chicken". Looks as if mom has already made up her mind, my mom shouted "PIZZA". Looking up with a shocking surprised my dad said "pizza it is".

Chapter 2

Understanding Me

Pulling up to the driveway at home, feeling exhausted and full from Smith's Pizzeria, all I could think about was how my day was at school. Everything seemed so perfect, that even after school I still felt butterflies from the conversations and text messages me and Charles have been exchanging all day. It was like a dream come true, "Dear, did you forget to let the dog out before we left?" My mom asked with a worried voice and a look on her face that could frighten a serial killer. "Think so!" I replied softly looking down at the ground, as we all began to head out the car and walked towards the house. "Woof, Woof, Woof." My dog barked happily scratching the front door as we entered the house. "So I guess you didn't let him out?" My mom said while looking through the house to make sure nothing was out of place and the dog didn't go on any of our new carpet or furniture we bought a couple weeks ago. "Alyssa, do you have any homework?" My dad asked yelling while he was the last one entering the house from cleaning out the car, bringing in the bags we had bought while eating dinner. "Alyssa!" My mom yelled while storming down the stairs with an angry face. "Your dog used the restroom all over our master bedroom and pulled down the blinds!" After taking a deep breath and swallowing hard, I replied, "I'll get it mom!" Thinking to myself that this is definitely the wrong time to ask if I could go out with Charles to the movies? "I bet you will!" My dad said with a straight face. Seeing that both of my parents were upset from not letting my dog out before we left, I figured I'd wait another day to ask.

Without a fight, I headed upstairs with a broom and dustpan to clean up the mess my dog made. While running up the stairs as my dog followed, I then got a text from Charles asking how my day was. I replied, "Fine, until now. I'm cleaning up the dog's mess he made while I was out with my parents." Charles replied, "Awwwww sounds fun! Lol" I then replied, "Yeah, it is smarty pants!" Standing on the bottom step, my mom yelled, "Are you almost done?!" With no hesitation, I replied, "Yeah! Sure mom!" I knew that if she was to come see the room, she would be upset that I hadn't done anything. Grabbing the broom and the dustpan, I quickly began sweeping and picking up what seemed to be shredded paper and dog waste. I put on my headphones to get my mind off cleaning, only to forget that Charles and I were still texting. Shortly after an hour gone by, I then began wrapping up and putting everything away. I looked at my phone, and seen that I had four text messages from Charles thinking that I had been ignoring him. With the last text stating that he was going to bed, I then replied, "Sorry! I was cleaning up and had my headphones on!" Screaming at the top of her lungs, my mom asked, "Are you finished Alyssa?!" Trying to match her scream, I replied, "Yes mom!" After putting up the broom and dustpan, I began getting ready for bed. While laying down, I then reached for my phone and seen I had four more texts! They were all from Charles. I replied to the last, "Sorry I been busy, if you want, feel free to call." Within seconds of the message I sent, Charles called. While whispering so my parents wouldn't hear, I answered, "Hi, Charles." He then replied, "Why haven't you replied to my texts?" Hearing his voice alone sent chills through my body. I replied, "Sorry, I was out with the family and cleaned as soon as I got home." Charles interrupted me with a serious tone, "Did you ask your parents about us going to the movies tomorrow?" Down and out, I replied, "Sorry, I wasn't able to, but I will tomorrow. Since it's the weekend I'm sure they wouldn't mind." Charles replied, "Ok, if anything keep me posted." I answered, "Well, it's getting kind of late, so I'll just talk to you tomorrow. Bye bye." Charles replied, "Goodbye".

After hanging up the phone, I fell fast asleep. "Ahhhhhh!" I woke feeling a sharp pain in my chest. My mother came running in barging through my door as if I was under attack. "What's wrong Alyssa?!" My mom asked while looking terrified. "I don't know mom! I have this sharp pain in my chest!" My mom asked, "Do you want me to call the doctor?!" I replied quickly, "No mom! If you could, get me an aspirin and a glass of water." Doing so, my mom quickly ran out the door, and headed straight to the bathroom. Looking at my phone, I seen I had six texts, all from Charles. All of them asked if I had talked to my parents about going to the movies with him. Setting my phone on the floor, my mom came back in. "Hun, how are you feeling?" I replied, "A little bit better" As she handed over the medicine and water I asked for. "Thanks mom." While feeling dizzy and sleepy, I slowly began to lie back down. While being awaken from the noisy alarm clock, I began getting ready for school. In the middle of getting ready, I realized the pain I once felt was gone. "Thank you Jesus!" I said to myself while running downstairs to my mom. She was next to the door with a lunch she packed for me. "Hey mom, this weekend I was wondering if I could go out with a friend of mine for a movie and maybe dinner." My mom answered, "Hmmm, we'll talk about it when you get home." Staring at the clock in the hall, it seemed this day was going by pretty fast. Already it was fifth period. Walking to class, I noticed Charles, but I didn't want him to notice me noticing him. I walked right into class with my books held to my chest tightly and head held low. I quickly sat down in my assigned seat. Feeling a slight tap on my shoulder, I slowly turned around, "Hey what's up?" It was Charles smiling hard as though he just won a million bucks. "Sooooo, did you ask your parents if it was ok for me to take you out this weekend?" I replied, "Well honestly, I asked my mom and she said we would talk about it as soon as I get home from school." Charles answered, "That's fine, just keep me posted." Feeling a slight pain in my chest again, I turned around and put my head on my desk. Charles asked, "Are you ok Alyssa?" I replied mumbling under my breath, "I'm fine, just a little tired, I didn't go to bed 'til late last night." Putting my head up, I tried to focus jotting down notes that was given in class. I glanced at the clock again, and already it was time to go.

While still feeling pain instead of going to my last class, I walked down to the nurse's office. As I began leaning on the lockers in the hall on my way there, I stopped at my locker to put my books away, knowing I will be spending the rest of my school day in the office. I then went on and checked in, "Good afternoon Alyssa! Is everything ok?" Says Nurse Valerie. "Yes, but no." I replied. "For some odd reason, while in class, I started to feel pain in my chest. It started late last night. While I was sleeping, the pain was so bad that it awoke me from sleeping." Nurse Valerie asked, "Have you taken any antibiotics or medications?" I replied, "Hmmmm, well I took a few aspirins, but that was late last night when I felt the pain, but it came back again." Looking kind of nervous and frightened, Nurse Valerie then asked, "Well dear, when was the last time you got a physical or had a checkup?" Thinking to myself, I then replied, "Wow, it's been a while!" "Well, to make sure that there isn't anything severely wrong, I will call and make an appointment for you in a week. Is that fine with you Alyssa?" While looking down feeling a little pain from my chest, I replied, "Ok, is there any medicine for my pain you can give me for the time being?" While handing me the aspirins, Valerie replied, "Well yes, and no problem." I looked at my watch seeing that I only had few minutes to go to my locker before I head home. Taking the medicine, I quickly got up and headed to my locker. Luckily, by the time I reached the school bus, my bus driver was still parked while talking on the phone.

Finally getting home, my dad asked, "How was your day dear, any pains?" Taking a deep breath, I said, "Yes". As I began to tell him how I spent the last couple hours of my day at the nurses office. "Oh wow, I'm so sorry to hear that." Looking down as if he was about to cry. "Any good news?" My dad asked. With a much brighter response, I answered, "Yes, indeed!" Switching the subject, I began to tell my dad, "Well, there's this guy friend I share a couple classes with, he has been asking me to go on this date with him, but it kept slipping my mind to ask you and mom if it was alright." While overhearing our conversation, my mom interrupted, "Ummm, Alyssa, who is this guy and please tell us about him. Looking at both of my parents with a straight face and confident smirk, I replied, "Well honestly, it's a guy from school, and his name is Charles. We have a couple classes together in school. He's nice and charming with a very cute smile." Loudly speaking, my dad said, "Soooo, when are we going to meet this Charles guy that you seem so in love with?" By the tone of his voice, he didn't want to hear me anymore. "Well, he asked me out a few days ago, but honestly, I was kind of hesitating and nervous to bring it up to you guys because I didn't know how you were going to react." Calmly speaking, my mom asked, "When is this special date?" I kind of smirked and answered, "It's actually tonight around seven or eightyish." My dad then asked, "So you will be missing dinner?" I replied, "Pretty much!" Giggling in my

20

response. "Then hun, it's best you start getting ready." My mother insisted. While rushing up the stairs, I quickly got in the shower and began to get ready. Rushing through my dresser trying to find a nice blouse to wear, the doorbell rang. "Mom! Dad! Can you please answer the door? I'll be down in a few, and I'm almost ready!" I said screaming at the top of my lungs. Racing to the door, my mom asked, "Who is it?" Charles politely responded, "Its Charles ma'am, I'm here to pick up Alyssa." Opening the door with a bright welcoming smile, "Hi, I'm Alyssa's mom, come right on in and have a seat on the couch; she will be down in a couple minutes. Can I get you anything?" Responding friendly to Charles. "No thank you." Charles replied feeling calm and relaxed. "I'm almost ready! I'll be down in a few!" I screamed yelling at the top of my lungs. While walking in from the kitchen door and gently greeting himself, my father says, "Hi, I'm Alyssa's father, you must be Charles, the guy Alyssa has told us so much about. Since I'm her father, I hope you don't mind me asking where you will be taking my daughter this evening." While sitting down looking at my dad nervously, Charles replied, "There's a nice restaurant on Maddison St. named Lawrence's Place. They serve pretty good food at a pretty good price." My dad replies, "Well Charles, if you need extra money to take my daughter out, let me know. I will give her a couple bucks just in case." Charles responds, "Well thanks sir, that'll be nice." Rushing down the stairs and heading towards the door, I greeted Charles, "Hi Charles, sorry for the wait, I hope my

mom and dad didn't harass you or make you feel uncomfortable."
With a smile, Charles replied, "Not at all, they were actually nice
and polite." "Well Alyssa, here's a couple extra dollars just in
case you guys come short of anything." I replied, "Thanks dad!"

While reaching in her purse, my mom says, "No no no, wait!"
She pulls out a Polaroid camera. "Let me take a picture before
you guys leave!" Yelling at the top of my voice, I said, "Mom!
That's so embarrassing!" Charles begins to giggle, "Ha ha ha,
that's fine, and it doesn't hurt to pose for a second." Quickly
snapping our picture, my mom says, "Say cheese! Ok, please be
safe and home by ten the latest!" While heading towards Charles
car out the door, I acknowledge my mom with a, "No problem!"
Looking at each other, my mom said quietly under her breath,
"Our baby girl is growing up so fast. I can't believe she's going
on her first date." While shaking his head, my dad says, "Me
either!"

Chapter 3

Loving Me.

Finally pulling up to the restaurant, Charles looked over at me and took a deep breath. "We're here!" he replied gently as if he was trying to surprise me, looking back with a smile, "Oh wow! This place brings back so many memories! I haven't been here in ages." I replied. While opening his door, "One moment, sit tight." As he quickly ran over to the passenger seat I was in and opened the door. "Wow, look at you being all nice, well thank you!" I said while trying to keep from blushing. Walking into the restaurant I couldn't stop looking or staring at how the place looked the same after all these years. "Hey Charles, that seat over there in the left corner was the seat me and my parents would always sit whenever we came here." I told Charles. At night, you could see the stars clearly and the ocean view sight is beautiful. "Well since you love it so much, why don't we sit over there?" Charles suggested. After we sat down, the waitress had come over with the menus. "Hi, my name is Ora. I will be your waitress for the day." She kindly explained. "Do you guys know what you want or do you need a second to decide?" While both looking through the menu, Charles and I said at the same time, "cheeseburgers please!" After looking at each other, we all began to laugh. "You guys are silly! Cheeseburgers it is!" The waitress agreed. "I'll be right back with your order." The waitress said as she walked away.

"So Alyssa, how was your day?" Charles asked. "Well to be honest with you, not so well. For some reason, I have been feeling nauseous and sharp pains in my chest. I talked to the school nurse and my parents, and they suggested I go to the hospital to make sure I'm ok. "Well have you gotten checked out?" Charles said with a serious look on his face. "Well... we did set an appointment but it's not till next week I believe. But as of now I'm ok." I replied unsurely. Looking at me with a blank stare on his face about to say something, "Here's your food!" The waitress interrupts with an exciting look on her face. "Will you guys need anything else?" Ora asked about to leave. "No thank you, we should be fine." Charles replied. Reaching for my drink, I began to feel the sharp pain in my chest I did while I was at school. "Oh my god," I said in so much pain trying not to make a scene. "Are you ok Alyssa?!" Charles asked with a nervous look on his face. "No, the pain is back, and it hurts more than before. Here, take my phone and call my dad." While dialing my dad's number, I slowly slumped down in my chair holding my chest as tears came rushing down my face. "Please Charles! Hurry!" I said weeping. "I am, I am", Charles answered back. After several rings, my dad finally answered the phone. "Hurry, Hurry! Alyssa's having really bad pains again!" Charles said nervously to my father. "Wait, what's wrong?! What happened?!" My dad said screaming over the phone. "She's in pain, really bad pain!

I'm going to take her to the hospital right now, please meet us there!" With no hesitation, my dad replied, "Ok, I'm on my way."

"Are you ok? I'm about to help you put your jacket on so we can go. The hospital isn't far from here." While slowly putting my jacket on and walking me to the car, Charles opened my door. "Here, take your time, and don't worry, I'll take care of you and make sure you're ok." With being in so much pain, hearing those words from a guy I secretly had a crush on, really made my heart melt. After finally pulling up to the hospital and being rushed through the emergency doors, I could only feel my chest tightening more and the pain began to feel worse. I started to feel my breath getting shorter and shorter each time I inhaled and exhaled. "How are you babe?" Charles said looking down at me. As I sat helplessly in pain in my wheelchair waiting to be called, "I'm fine, just in a lot of pain right now." I slowly replied. "Thanks so much for being here with me by my side through all this, it really means a lot." "No problem Alyssa." Charles said while looking out the window as though he had a lot on his mind. "Everything is going to be alright." He repeated while turning around walking towards me. I could start to feel the intensity between us while still in pain. While reaching over and putting his soft, gentle hands over mine, "Look, even if it means me spending the night here, I will make sure you are well taken care of. I…" "Alyssa!" The intercom said my name interrupting Charles. "The nurse is ready to see you." With no hesitation,

Charles quickly began to stroll me in my wheelchair as the nurse carefully guided me to my room. "Here is your room, a doctor should be here shortly to come in and talk to you guys." While finally having a moment to ourselves, we stared at each other as tears rolled down our faces. Strolling towards Charles, I softly reached over to wipe the tears from his eyes. "Thank you." I said while giving him a hug so tight, that god could not separate us. Opening the door, the doctor came in, "Hi, you must be Alyssa." While turning his head looking at Charles asking, "And you are?" With a straight face Charles quickly replied, "I'm Charles, Alyssa's boyfriend",as he shook the doctor's hand. "Oh how sweet." The doctor said before turning and looking at me with a serious face. "Well Alyssa, from what I'm hearing about what you're going through, I would like to take a few tests and x rays to make sure your body is up and running." Replying nervously, I answered, "That's fine." "It will be a moment before we can do all that, but I must warn you, we have to admit you here, and have you stay overnight." Shaking my head, I agreed, "That's fine. Hey Charles, if you can, please grab my phone out my jacket and update my parents on what's going on with me." "No need to." Charles replied. "I have told them everything and your parents are on their way." Looking at the clock, "Excuse me doctor, what time will the x rays and everything begin?" "Momentarily." He replied. Opening the door was a nurse whose name tag I could barely read because of her long beautiful hair covering it. "Hi, you must be Alyssa, I am Nurse Patty. You look so pretty today, you guys coming from a date?" As me and Charles looked at each other and quietly giggled, "Well yea, sort of." I replied. "Well I will be your nurse for the day, and I will now take you to get your tests and X rays done." Looking at Charles, Nurse Patty suggested, "Excuse me sir, would you like to come?" "Well no thanks, honestly I'd rather wait here for Alyssa's parents to show up." "Ok that's fine." Nurse Patty replied as she wheeled me off to the x ray room.

As we began to enter the x ray room, the sharp pain in my chest began to get worse. "Ms. Patty, please help." I almost begged. You could tell by my facial expression that I was in a lot of pain. "Help Ms. Patty, help!" I repeated as the pain in my chest began to ache more and more. "Ok Alyssa, we just need to take these x rays to find out exactly what's wrong with you." While sitting on the x ray table holding my chest, I noticed a slight small bump on my left breast each time I inhaled and exhaled. While being x rayed, feeling sluggish and exhausted, you could tell by my posture that I was in a lot of pain. "Are we almost done Ms. Patty? Please say yes." I asked with a gentle but little giggle. "Yes, we are almost done in fact. Just a couple more and you'll be back in your room in no time." Having finished the tests and headed back to the room, I hear a familiar and dramatic voice scream, "Alyssa! Alyssa! Are you ok?! Is everything fine?!" Turning around in my wheel chair, it was my parents. As we all headed back to the room, my dad asked, "Nurse, how is she? Is everything fine?" As Nurse Patty lifted her head and slightly looked at my dad with a worried but serious facial expression, "Honestly sir, we will be giving you the tests results any minute now. But from what Alyssa has explained to me, it might look like it could be something serious, but we won't know until we get the results back." Having finally arrived to my room, I noticed Charles seemed very stressed and worried. While rocking back and forth sitting on my hospital bed, "Are you ok babe?" I asked while rolling towards him in my wheelchair. "No!" He said as tears gently came down his eyes. His voice began to slowly crack as if he was going to cry. While holding his hands and reaching for him, I began to shed tears as well. "I'm going to be ok. Don't you worry about me; I'm going to be fine." Lifting his head up and using his left pointer finger to lift my chin, he then pulled his face close to mine as his soft warm lips gently kissed mine. "Awwww." My mom said as tears began running down her face. Walking through the door to my surprise was Nurse Patty. She had papers in her hands which seemed to be the results from the x ray tests. "Well, to be perfectly honest with you guys, I would like you all to sit down together. I have some very shocking news that I think you should be prepared for."

With a straight face I answered, "Well, let us know what's going on?" Ms. Patty replied as she licked her fingers thumbing through the papers, "Well first of all, while going over the x ray tests, the doctors found out that Alyssa has breast cancer." My mom and dad then started to scream, "Noooo!" Holding my head down, Charles then began to put his arms around me. "I can't believe this! God, why me?" I said as I began to break down in tears. "But…" Replied Ms. Patty as she interrupted my plea to God. "You're only in your second stage, which means it's still early, and I'm glad you came when you did before it spreaded." "So there is hope?" My mom asked. "Yes, there is, so don't be so quick to throw in the towel just yet." Replied Nurse Patty. With a smile on her face, nurse Patty explained, "I already set up a time for Alyssa to have surgery tomorrow morning." While wiping the tears from his eyes, my mother praised, "Thank you so much! Knowing we came just in time shows god does work in mysterious ways and that our guardian angels are watching over us." "Well, I will be leaving you guys alone so you can be together. There will be a nurse or someone that will get Alyssa for surgery tomorrow morning." Nurse Patty said while opening the door and leaving the room. "Everything is going to be alright. We just have to pray that my surgery goes as planned." I told Charles and my parents. Looking over at Charles, I slightly rolled over to him lifting up his head. "I really want to thank you for being here for me." "Yes thanks a lot Charles. We're glad you decided to take her immediately when she had the pain." My parents said agreeing with me. While wiping the tears from his eyes, Charles answered, "No problem, I would have done anything to help Alyssa." While playing board games to get our minds off this stressful day, I hadn't realized how quick time had passed as the sun began to rise. Before I knew it, a nurse knocked on my door, "Alyssa, are you ready? It's time for your big day."

While still feeling exhausted from staying up, I looked at the nurse and took a deep breath, I replied, "Yes." "Are you going to be ok?" Charles replied. "Yes, I'll be ok, you guys just stay here, and I'll be back in no time." I said as I began to leave. While slowly being pushed off to begin surgery, Charles told me in the sweetest tone, "I love you." As surgery was beginning, the doctor placed a mask on my face, and I began to fall asleep. As I woke up in my room, I looked at my parents and Charles and began to think. I have never felt more loved and safe in my life. No matter the insecurities, doubts, or health issues, I will always have my family, faith and God. I will remain grateful because I have understood that life is shorter than you think, especially when you least expect it. We take a lot of things for granted in this life, wanting all of the beautiful things, but it really is the beauties within that people really want.

Chapter 4

Poems

Inner Beauty

Written by: Neme Cancel

A beauty within is not judged by the color of her skin

It's not the curve in her waist

The prettiness in her face

How many heart breaks can one take?

Or how hard your booty can shake

But instead how about trying to embrace ones mistake

Because nowadays everyone can be easily replaced

We all come in different shapes and sizes

But get caught up trying to figure out what the prize is

So we cover our flaws with makeup, tattoos and even disguises

The sky's the limit that's what we're often told

Trying to figure out the difference between hot and cold

Speak up because even the toughest are not as bold

Try and stay on path and create your own road

Feeling the weight on your shoulders

And can barely hold your own load

But the inner strength is overpowering

And you realize you would never fold

"Lesson's Embraced"

Written by: Quinn De' Leon

As I look at my reflection.

Visible scars, natural beauty imperfection.

Passed flaws and mistakes from life's misdirection's.

Walking numb and heartless from all rejections.

False promises, more like convinced hypothesis.

Daze in traumas got to come back to consciousness.

Make up my soul some self-confidence.

Rejuvenating my thoughts but guilty of all evidence.

Never thought I'd be marked due to relationship negligence.

34